A Note to Parents and Caregivers:

Read-it! Readers are for children who are just starting on the amazing road to reading. These beautiful books support both the acquisition of reading skills and the love of books.

 The PURPLE LEVEL presents basic topics and objects using high frequency words and simple language patterns.

 The RED LEVEL presents familiar topics using common words and repeating sentence patterns.

 The BLUE LEVEL presents new ideas using a larger vocabulary and varied sentence structure.

 The YELLOW LEVEL presents more challenging ideas, a broad vocabulary, and wide variety in sentence structure.

 The GREEN LEVEL presents more complex ideas, an extended vocabulary range, and expanded language structures.

 The ORANGE LEVEL presents a wide range of ideas and concepts using challenging vocabulary and complex language structures.

When sharing a book with your child, read in short stretches, pausing often to talk about the pictures. Have your child turn the pages and point to the pictures and familiar words. And be sure to reread favorite stories or parts of stories.

There is no right or wrong way to share books with children. Find time to read with your child, and pass on the legacy of literacy.

Adria F. Klein, Ph.D.
Professor Emeritus
California State University
San Bernardino, California

First American edition published in 2005 by
Picture Window Books
5115 Excelsior Boulevard
Suite 232
Minneapolis, MN 55416
877-845-8392
www.picturewindowbooks.com

First published in Canada in 1999 by
Les éditions Héritage inc.
300 Arran Street, Saint Lambert
Quebec, Canada J4R 1K5

Printed in the United States of America.

Library of Congress Cataloging-in-Publication Data
Tremblay, Carole, 1959-
Emily Lee / author: Carole Tremblay ; illustrator: Stéphane Jorisch.
p. cm. — (Read-it! readers)
Summary: Emily Lee is a seven-year-old witch who, because of her confusion about left and right, accidentally turns herself into a toaster.
ISBN 1-4048-1077-3 (hardcover)
[1. Witches—Fiction.] I. Jorisch, Stéphane, ill. II. Title. III. Series.

PZ7.T1927Em 2005
[E]—dc22
2004024892

Emily Lee

By Carole Tremblay
Illustrated by Stephane Jorisch

Special thanks to our advisers for their expertise:

Adria F. Klein, Ph.D.
Professor Emeritus, California State University
San Bernardino, California

Susan Kesselring, M.A.
Literacy Educator
Rosemount - Apple Valley - Eagan (Minnesota) School District

PICTURE WINDOW BOOKS
Minneapolis, Minnesota

Emily Lee is seven. She has fair skin and rosie cheeks. She doesn't look that different from you and me.

Emily's mother is a witch. Her father is a witch. Her sister, Julia, is a witch. Her brothers, Nathan and Ted, are witches. This means, of course, that Emily is also a witch.

In this family of witches, everyone is nice and polite. No warts on their noses, no spider webs under their arms, no spiders in the cookie dough.

All of this does not prevent Emily from doing silly things. Just like all the little girls in the world, she likes to play tricks on her brothers and sister. She also loves to do what her mom does. The problem is, Emily Lee is too young to do magic tricks.

Emily Lee has trouble telling her left from her right. And her right from her left. That kind of mistake, with a magic wand, can cause big problems.

That's exactly what happened the other day.
Emily's brother, Ted, was watching television.
As a joke, Emily hid behind the sofa. She tried
to change the television into a toaster.

She took her mother's wand and said,
"Chica-chica-cadabra-bam!"

Emily knew that she had to hold her wand with her right hand in order for the spell to work. When she was the one who got transformed into a toaster, she knew she made a big mistake! She had been holding her wand in her left hand.

Ted did not notice anything. He kept watching his favorite program. Zing! Pang! Slam! The aliens were getting smashed on television. Ted stayed still.

Emily did, too, because a moving toaster is pretty rare, don't you think?

At six o'clock, their mother shouted, "Time to eat everyone!"

Ted grabbed the remote control saying, "Abracadabra-cha-cha-cha." He turned off the TV. He likes to pretend the remote control is a magic wand.

Mrs. Lee was serving the chicken soup when she suddenly asked, "Where could Emily be?" Nobody knew. She shouted, "Emily?"

No answer. Mrs. Lee frowned,"Emily?"

Emily was no where to be seen.

She grabbed Pat, the baby saying, "Well, dinner is delayed, my dears. We have to find Emily."

15

Mrs. Lee, Ted, Keith, Julia, and Pat got up from the table. Mr. Lee was still in his truck driving home.

"What in the world did she change herself into this time?" whispered Julia.

This was not Emily's first mistake with magic. One day, wanting to bother Keith while he was doing his homework, she accidentally transformed herself into a purple ink pen. She spent the whole evening in the school box. Ted found her while looking for his stapler.

Another morning, Emily tried to change her sister's toothbrush into a flyswatter. Julia realized what was happening as soon as the flyswatter landed on her foot.

As always, Mrs. Lee led the search. She sent Keith to the basement, Julia to the attic, and Ted to the yard. She would inspect the main floor with Pat.

The search began immediately.

"Emily, is that you?" Julia asked a lamp.

"Are you in there, Emily?" asked Keith, talking to a rake.

"Come on, get out of there," whispered Ted to an old rug.

If a stranger walked into the house right then, they would have thought that something was wrong with the family.

Mrs. Lee was walking through the bedrooms and hallways at a fast pace. First, she had to find her magic wand. She knew the little witch would not be too far from it.

"Emily, is that you?"

"Go on, Pat, try to find Mommy's wand!" she said to the baby who was crawling under the dresser.

Mr. Lee walked into the house. The whole family rushed when they heard the door slam.

They all shouted out, "Emily, is that you?"

"She disappeared again?" Dad asked, looking concerned.

"We looked everywhere!" said Ted.

"From the basement to the attic!" added Keith.

"Even under the staircase!" replied Julia.

Pat, who everybody had forgotten about, came in the room pulling a toaster by the cord.

"Emmie all gone?" he babbled in his
baby language.

"I asked you to get my magic wand, Pat, not
the electric toaster," Mrs. Lee said smiling. She
turned to Julia, "Would you put that away?"

"Yes, mom," Julia replied.

Just as Julia was putting her hand on the
toaster, it started shooting out crumbs, like
a volcano erupting.

Mom looked at Dad, who looked at Julia, who looked at Keith, who looked at Pat.

"Emily?" sighed Mrs. Lee. "OK, my dear, show me where you left my wand. Otherwise, I won't be able to change you back into a little girl."

The toaster's cord slowly wiggled on the floor.
When it stopped, it was pointing toward
the sofa.

"I'll get it," said Ted.

He came back with the wand, and Mrs. Lee
cast the spell, "Ripe banana, click and clack—
bring your own bright face back!"

Emily appeared in front of the whole family.
She was scratching her back with her hands.
"Ouch! I have crumbs in my dress," she said.

"Emily," said her dad, "promise me you will
not go to bed before knowing your right from
your left."

Emily raised her hand and said, "I promise!"

The following morning, Emily repeated, "Left is that way. Right is that way."

"Bravo!" cheered Mrs. Lee.

But, when looking at the little witch's shoes, which were on the wrong feet, Mr. Lee realized they would still have to keep an eye on her.

More *Read-it!* Readers

Bright pictures and fun stories help you practice your reading skills. Look for more books at your level.

A Clown in Love by Mireille Villeneuve
Alex and the Game of the Century by Gilles Tibo
Alex and Toolie by Gilles Tibo
Daddy's an Alien by Bruno St-Aubin
Emily Lee Carole Temblay
Forrest and Freddy by Gilles Tibo
Gabby's School by the Sea by Marie-Danielle Croteau
Grampy's Bad Day by Dominique Demers
John's Day by Marie-Francine Hébert
Peppy, Patch, and the Postman by Marisol Sarrazin
Peppy, Patch, and the Socks by Marisol Sarrazin
The Princess and the Frog by Margaret Nash
Rachel's Adventure Ring by Sylvia Roberge Blanchet
Run! by Sue Ferraby
Sausages! by Anne Adeney
Stickers, Shells, and Snow Globes by Dana Meachen Rau
Theodore the Millipede by Carole Tremblay
The Truth About Hansel and Gretel by Karina Law
When Nobody's Looking ... by Louise Tondreau-Levert

Looking for a specific title or level? A complete list of *Read-it!* Readers is available on our Web site:
www.picturewindowbooks.com